ALEXANDRE KOSTOLIAS

Rio's big blast

ALEXANDRE KOSTOLIAS

Rio's big blast

Credits

© Jaguatirica, 2019 All rights reserved.

Library of Congress – United States Copyright Office
Control Number: 1-4797284781

Title: Rio's Big Blast – Living in 2065
Author: Alexandre Kostolias

Adapted, expanded and freely translated by the author from the original Portuguese language edition of the sci-fi story entitled "o quinto centenário" ("the fifth centennial"), in "Rio em seis tempos", by Alexandre Kostolias, editora Jaguatirica, Rio de Janeiro, 2015 conceived, expanded and adapted by Alexandre Kostolias this edition published in 2017 by Editora Jaguatirica, Rio de Janeiro, Brazil. Planet Earth version

publisher Paula Cajaty
digital publishing 54 Design
cover design Rodrigo Herzog
revised Robert Bozina and Alexandre Kostolias
Issued in electronic and printed format.

ISBN 978-989-8938-56-5

GATO BRAVO
rua de Xabregas 12, lote A, 276-289
1900-440 Lisboa, Portugal
tel. [+351] 308 803 682
editoragatobravo@gmail.com

editoragatobravo.pt

Content

Rio's Big Blast: Living in 2065

THE YEAR IS 2065. RIO DE JANEIRO, BRAZIL, is getting ready to celebrate its 500th anniversary. Ten million people will attend the event at the giant Copacabana Beach Park. Billions will watch on colossal screens spread throughout the Solar System. However, at midnight, something unprecedented and bombastic will, and is about to happen.

Bruna is perhaps the last human female of her species who wants to be loved, wants to be a mother, and who wants to love and nurture her own children. Her civil cohabitant Maxim is too busy piloting spaceships to and from Planet Mars to offer her any attention. Bruna fears he's, at least in part, an android.

An immersion into what things will be like living in Rio, living in Brazil, living on planet Earth, living on the Moon, and living on other planets in the Solar System.

More significantly, this is an essay that seeks to address the overwhelming, startling, and unavoidable issue of whom and what we human beings will have become by 2065.

About the Author

ALEXANDRE KOSTOLIAS WAS BORN IN RIO DE JANEIRO, Brazil, in 1949. He lived his early years and part of his adult life in the United States, mostly in San Francisco, California. He travelled to over forty countries in the Americas, Europe, North Africa and Asia. He graduated in International Relations (Magna cum Laude, 1985) from San Francisco State University and attended the University of California, Berkeley. Later, back to Rio, he published four books in Portuguese, including two novels.

Alexandre Kostolias sees himself as a Brazilian writer who aspires to become a citizen of the world and believes that "there is no road map to peace, that peace is the road map", a habit, a culture, a way of coexisting.

We just belong to a small planet lost in the universe.

***

Rio's big blast – living in 2065 , a sci-fi story, is the
author's first book (e-book version) published in English
and is an adaptation and enlargement of his futuristic
short story "O quinto centenário" (translates as "The fifth
centennial"), included in the book "Rio em seis tempos",
published by editora Jaguatirica, Rio de Janeiro, 2015.

to Alessandra

One

EMERGING FROM THE DEPTHS OF THE LAGOON[1] in her Speedam LX Chameleon, Bruna1431KL was glamorous and smartly dressed. The Speedam, a third generation electrically powered air, surface and submarine transport vehicle displayed black and yellow stripes on its panels. Black and yellow were the perfect colors for heavy traffic. Speedily moving into the RB[2] (#2) III Tunnel, Bruna1431KL heard the double *beep* generated by the toll machine indicating it had charged her Monthly Transit Account. She knew the charge was to be 200 New Reais (about 100 US$).

Heading toward Tom Jobim Spaceport (TJSP) at 250 km (160 mph) an hour, the vehicle levitated magnetically and nearly touched the titanium rails of the RB III Tunnel. Like all vehicles transiting the tunnel, the Speedam was self-driving and interacted with the immediate environment. As long as systems didn't malfunction, the tunnel was free from vehicle crashes. Regrettably, at times

---

1   Lagoa is a natural lagoon located in the middle of Rio de Janeiro's prestigious South Zone, a coastal area, and is surrounded by residential neighborhoods.

2   RB stands for Rebouças, the name of the tunnel that connects Rio's South Zone with the North Zone

systems did malfunction. But according to Bruna's Sphynx on-board oracle this wouldn't happen today; a smooth ride was forecasted. Also according to Sphynx, she would overfly the spaceport's vicinity in 3 minutes and 37 seconds. However, also according to her oracle, as soon as she reached massive TJSP, her self-driving (and self-parking) car would waste 54 minutes trying to find parking space before it docked itself in the 20-story underground parking lot.

– *Sh%$##!*, she moaned in anticipated frustration, while retouching her Perenial27 make up, prepared with Rejuvenium, a skin-regenerating substance. It was brought in from planet Mars by Bruna's *civil cohabitant*, Maxim3131ZX.

Maxim was a spaceship pilot in the recently opened Riosp-Mars space shuttle. TJSP was one of the 12 locations in the planet, the only one in the ULATAM (União Latino Americana, a Latin American Confederation) from where space voyages departed. Other spaceports were located in New York, Las Vegas, Singapore, Shanghai, Okinawa, Moscow, Nice, London, Mumbai, Dubai and Johannesburg. A few more were under construction.

Score one for Riosp, an immense conurbation of 40 million people that included the former metropolitan areas of Rio de Janeiro and São Paulo (Sampario had been another name option for the megalopolis, but it was decided that Riosp had more touristic appeal).

Both ends of Riosp were now completely integrated by 18 main lines of High-Speed Metro plus a number of branch lines. Therefore, passengers who boarded the Central Subway Station in São Paulo, built uphill and far away from the coast, could reach Ipanema Beach Station, in Rio, in exactly 34 minutes. The *paulistas'* (São Paulo dwellers) long-awaited dream of a quick ride to the beach did finally come true.

Meanwhile, a *Magway* composed of 22 magnetic levitation lanes for all sorts of vehicles, gave access to a mega touristic region along the Green Coast, featuring about 600 resorts and 6000 inns.

Trips to Mars were the planetary buzz of 2065. Package tours to the Moon, less exclusive and much less expensive, were still popular in people's imagination. But truly sophisticated couples were no longer impressed by those "Honeymoon on the Moon!" travel industry sleazy ads which had been the planetary craze only 20 years before.

The Moon had become nothing but a frantic nightmare, with its colossal casinos entertaining innumerable amounts of customers in every imaginable way. Many gamblers systematically won millions of *astrodollars* (the currency used on the Moon and some planets of the Solar System) at late night just to lose every *astropenny* before breakfast. Many enjoyed the excitement of having become fake millionaires for a few hours. Others found the frustration of having lost all their "fortunes" too hard to bear and would commit suicide in front of an applauding crowd by shooting themselves. With fake bullets, of course, so nobody got hurt. *That* was regarded as top entertainment. The whole idea was to provide high-adrenalin amusement to masses that lived their daily lives in a permanent state of boredom.

In addition, there was a wide choice of lunar extravaganza options, from 5 star, highly luxurious shopping malls catering to pampered, narcissistic consumers, to honeymooners' love nests of all kinds. There were even sexual fantasies' theme parks.

Lunar entertainment developers had built not only gigantic casinos, but also many non-gambling businesses such as *no-drugs-banned* convenience stores, *intelligent drugs' spas*, destination-wedding facilities, vintage rock shows in 4 dimensions, and *demented rapture* concerts, for those who chose to go irreversibly insane.

In strictly technical terms, a trip to the Moon was a very simple matter, it's so nearby. On the other hand, an all-inclusive package tour to Mars had to wait a few more years. Now, it had become yet another product offered by the travel industry.

It was only after nuclear fusion was mastered and safely employed in space crafts that trips to Mars became commercially feasible. Combined with the development of magnetic technology and the use of gravitational forces, the new technology was a game changer, an outstanding breakthrough in interplanetary navigation. It freed humankind from remaining restricted to the Solar System; it emancipated humans from the isolation of Solar System confinement.

In 2065 travel time between planet Earth and either to Liberty Mars Spaceport, leased by NASA to a multinational corporation, or to the Russian-Chinese Gagarin New Beijing Cosmodrome, an inter-governmental joint venture, had been reduced to a mere 12 Earth hours. It was even possible to diminish the actual cruising time of the journey between the Blue Planet and the Red Planet in case of emergency. But it wasn't advisable: 12 hours was the bare minimum time in commercial flights for interplanetary acclimatization. It was essential to adapt visitors to the specific conditions of planet Mars, and it was prudent not to aggravate the disturbing consequences of *space lag.*

Two

WHEN BRUNA WAS JUST ABOUT TO GET OFF the city tunnel, she took a quick look at the cabin's display panel, a miracle (or perhaps a nightmare) of digital technology. With a quick facial contraction, she moved her left ear lobe slightly downward turning off her implanted *wise phone*. Bruna couldn't stand any longer the uninterrupted flow of incoming calls, either commercial or personal, that she got 24 by 7. No wonder, Bruna had about 7 million virtual friends spread over hundreds of social network groups from different planets. Paradoxically, in her everyday life, Bruna wasn't sure she could count seven *real* friends.

She also became fidgety for having to sit pretty on the driver´s seat and do absolutely nothing but retouch her make up. Self-driving cars were *sooo* boring.

As she was finally getting off the tunnel and her vehicle was gaining momentum on the take-off ramp, Bruna switched the car's operational mode back to manual driving and felt a sensation of immediate relief. Following instructions she had received from the Urban Traffic controllers, she made the vehicle ascend to the 1900 feet level sky lane and through a voice command she accelerated it to 480 km (300 miles) an hour. She felt mighty, she felt empowered. Wow, what a feeling!

Bruna1431KL was a licensed real estate broker dealing with housing projects on the Moon. She was a typical *carioca* (people born in Rio de Janeiro) in many ways. Fun-loving, impatient and, at times, temperamental, Bruna was passionate about everything she did.

She reset the Chameleon photosensitive vehicle's outer body panel to display the recently-adopted Brazilian flag; Maxim disapproved the new version. While keeping the green field and the yellow quadrangular rhombus, the rather old-fashioned national motto "Order and Progress" had to go in these *neo politically-correct* times. The motto had been substituted by "Human-Humanoid Rights and Sustainable Development", both much more 21st century-like. Also, every 10 seconds the motto's band would cheerfully display for a second the expression "VIVA ULATAM" on both sides of the flag. The idea behind all this display flashing was to reassure the country's commitment to continental integration. All those haphazardly assembled stars and constellations of the old banner also had to go as they were almost impossible to reproduce with precision. The only remaining stars in the new flag were the Southern Cross, symbolizing the Southern Hemisphere, below the display band, and the Polar Star, above it, representing the Northern Hemisphere.

Brazil, after all, is located in both hemispheres. It had increased further its northern hemisphere domains with the purchase of French Guiana for the astronomical amount of 90 trillion Euros, paid with revenues obtained from the ultra-deep South Atlantic oil extraction.

Even though fossil fuels had been substituted by other more efficient and less polluting sources of energy, the demand for synthetic resins had increased manifold.

In 2065, entire residential blocks were mass-built in a few hours thanks to giant 3D mammoth printers fed by rivers of resin mixed with biomass. Housing units were quickly assembled by robots at very low cost. This, combined with lower birthrate indexes, had contributed to improve dwellers' conditions in most of ULATAM's political units. In some regions there was actually a housing glut, with supply largely exceeding demand.

Deep water oceanic exploration had become a national obsession. Drilling oil 50 km (about 35 mi) below the ocean floor had finally become technically and economically viable. There was an ocean of oil underneath the Atlantic Ocean.

Regrettably, all this drilling came true at a very high environmental cost. Búzios (a beach resort North of Rio de Janeiro) had become, for a few years, one of the most polluted places on Earth in the aftermath of an ecological disaster of cataclysmic dimensions.

One of the most beautiful seashores on Earth became a coastline of gooey tar beaches and the whole marine ecosystem was affected. It took about 20 years to repair the damage. Flotillas of ocean cleanup vessels piloted by smart robots were used at an enormous cost which was never disclosed; it became a well-kept state secret.

"There is no free lunch", politicians and technocrats would reply to any criticism. Every benefit – Brazil had become one of the wealthiest nations on Earth – always entails a cost. "And sometimes things *do* get out of hand".

Social inequality had remained remarkably high, despite millions of housing units that were practically handed out for free through populist governmental programs. But easily available housing was not enough to promote social advancement, much more was needed.

Higher investments in education should have been made. Unfortunately, learning wasn't given very high priority by successive national administrations.

Quality education in public high schools and universities had made very little progress over the past 50 years.

One hindrance to quality education was that public universities had remained for many years tuition-free for the students. To many, it sounded as a good idea. However, a chronic scarcity of public funding for education was the norm; most universities became dysfunctional and pathetically outdated in educational and technological terms. After all, state of the art labs and libraries, modern classrooms, digital equipment and artificial intelligence units are very expensive to build and maintain.

On the other hand, private universities (including the Brazilian branches of highly prestigious American institutions such as Harvard, Yale, Columbia and Stanford) were way too expensive for the vast majority of students. Thus, even though money could buy high-quality education in Brazil, it wasn't for everyone; social inequality had remained a major issue.

Corrective measures were attempted with scant success. A system of quotas in which low-performing students were given preference in public universities' enrollment over top-grade ones, all in name of equality and social justice, backfired. Students began to do reverse cheating; A-level students began to mark the wrong answers on purpose in order to qualify for enrollment. While Brazil pursued on its erratic educational path there was a severe shortage of highly skilled specialists in the workforce. This type of human capital had to be imported from abroad (mainly from Europe, where millions of humans with Master's Degrees and PhD's were making home-delivery of pizzas and fries) together with many thousands of proletarian androids.

To aggravate things, the artificial intelligence revolution had become a threat for those humans who weren't particularly skilled or highly qualified. Widespread employment of robots in the agricultural, industrial and service sectors had simply made hundreds of millions of workers redundant.

The substitution of humans by robots in the workforce had triggered a major planetary crisis. Things didn't get even worse simply because in most wealthy nations (including Brazil) the number of people over 65 was larger than the quantity of those under 18 and therefore, relatively few people were entering the job market. Also, life-expectancy had risen considerably in most nations.

The UN and the UP, after discussing for many years all matters related to labor and demographics, voted for the adoption of part-time working hours for the entire planet, except for the Failed States of the World, where all labor activities were either illicit or downright criminal.

In order to reduce chronic unemployment, five-hour daily schedules (or twenty-hour weekly schedules) had become the norm for most workers. To most humans work meant to watch robots do their jobs and to report any irregularities to their bosses, at times also an artificial intelligence system.

Consequently, there was an awful lot of spare time. Wages weren't too high but manufactured goods in general were less costly than before. Not surprisingly, leisure had become one of the most important industries in the planetary new economy.

Two thousand years before, the Roman Empire had been a part-time civilization, with most activities open only until midday (presumably, at least for the non-slave population). In the afternoon, many, if not most Romans indulged in recreational activities either at the public baths, at the Coliseum or at the other circuses spread throughout the Empire. They spent most of their idle time rooting for their favorite gladiators or charioteers, shouting, talking, eating and drinking.

By 2065, having the androids replaced the slaves from antiquity the world had become once again a part-time civilization. And the privileged were still a minority.

By then, a mere junior analyst position in a magnetic – gravitational rail plant required from the candidate a Ph.D. in Transportation Engineering besides innumerable certifications. Thirty years of intensive formal education (now called *Human Learning*) were expected in order to qualify the candidate for any professional position. Many babies were enrolled in pre-elementary schools at the age of 3 *months*.

Among the privileged few who inhabited the planet, only an even more selected few had earned Cosmic Magnetic Gravitational Certificates (CMG's). Both Bruna and Maxim had received these highly-prized credentials, issued by the United Planets Organization (UP) after passing intensive world-wide CMG exams. It entitled them to exercise their respective careers anywhere in the Solar System.

In order to compensate the underprivileged, those who had been all but uncared for when it came down to receiving their fair share of the new national bonanza, a series of social programs had been devised, essentially to give the people "bread and circus" and keep them from complaining about life. The most popular of these programs was Calorie Care, which allowed all Brazilian citizens to *"pork out"* at any licensed fast-food establishment of his or her choice. To offset the millions of obese citizens this program had brought about, another widely publicized scheme was implemented, Fit Care: thousands of licensed gyms were opened to keep ULATAM citizens in good shape. Besides, the distribution free tickets for soccer games became a common practice.

At the same time France, now merely an Autonomous State in the EF, the European Federation, was in dire straits. It had to find funding to cover its social programs' colossal costs, which entitled the French people to the Human Right of Socialist Gastronomy. Celebrated restaurants such as La Tour d'Argent were now huge, ever-crowded franchised establishments catering to citizens enjoying gourmet State subsidies. They spent hours busily devouring tons of *Paté de Foie Gras* and piles of *Canard à l'Orange* accompanied by the finest wines from Bordeaux and Burgundy.

The acquisition of French Guiana (now re-named Guiana Caiena), plus the adoption of a new flag had both been proposed by Brazil's president and ULATAM'S co-General Secretary, Professor Big Lou (or in Portuguese, Professor Luizão). The purchase had been approved by Direct Digital Democracy (DDD), the online democratic direct-consultation system adopted by the country. DDD had replaced the utterly discredited National Congress and all political parties had been abolished. Thousands of politicians, at city, state and federal levels, as well as their innumerable assistants, had lost their jobs forever. Who needed them, anyway?

Maxim was indifferent to politics, but not to style. He didn't approve the changes in the national flag. He said it looked very confusing. He liked everything simple and clean. He would rather have all bands and stars removed, just leaving a big empty royal blue circle right in the middle of the flag. *That* would look clean and stylish.

Bruna, who felt very Solar-Systemic (as opposed to nationalistic or Earth-centric) in her allegiances, couldn't care less about the flag and just wanted to tease Maxim. She knew he disliked the new flag's design and just wanted to watch him getting annoyed. Or, at least, to see him laughing or feeling any form of emotion. She kept trying to stir him up, but always got frustrated and, at times, frightened. He seemed to be so coldly rational, so eerily devoid of any human feeling...

From his perspective, though, Maxim saw things very differently.

Born to be an orphan, he was the result of a genetic experiment funded by AlphaGen, a renowned *multi planetary* biopharmaceutical corporation headquartered on the Moon.

On the Moon human engineering was questioned by the UN and the UP but sporadically allowed amid enormous controversy. There, labs could breed people to become super humans on an experimental basis.

Maxim was the result of one such experiment. His genes were carefully selected from highly-qualified donor material. He was scientifically engineered by a secret committee of scientists working under the supervision of an even more secret committee director to produce a superior form of human species.

Maxim, having no parents, was raised at the AlphaGen Human Development Center on the Moon, where he was submitted from age 3 (3 months!) to a highly compacted program of Accelerated Learning designed to stimulate his intelligence to the very highest level.

His experiment mates, 4 females and 3 males, plus he, for total of 8 super humans were assisted by a number of professors, teachers and coaches. Not to speak of the dozens of androids who catered to all their needs.

They all lived in some sort of luxury resort that included sports facilities of many kinds. After they became officially adults, at age 18, they received, on a strict performance-related basis, passes to indulge in committee-approved entertainment. After all, they lived on the Moon. Nevertheless, any grade less than an A meant that they were grounded in their individual luxury cells. No wonder they were all too anxious to graduate and join the *real worlds* at age 25. After graduation they could stay on the Moon if they pleased, or could move to Earth or to any planet they cared to inhabit.

It was a lonely life. Maxim could hardly call his mates friends: all of them were permanently competing with each other; high-pressure learning and intense competition were part of the fundamentals of the experiment.

Over the years, they (officially named the Experimentals) were educated, indoctrinated and constantly tested on subjects such as math skills, logical reasoning, problem-solving abilities, lateral thinking, quantitative analysis, fuzzy math, physical geography (planetary, galactic and universal), on twelve languages spoken on planet Earth, quantum astronomy, and hundreds of scientific theories.

Very little was taught in terms of humanities and social sciences; practically not a word about history, philosophy, psychology or sociology. Not a note about music. The committee had decided that no teaching that might lead the Experimentals to question either their lives or the Established Truth should be encouraged.

Everybody in the committee pretended to stand for Freedom, Democracy, Liberty, Equality and Fraternity (hmm, not really, this last ideal had been officially deleted from the corporate set of beliefs). But questioning the Established Truth just didn't go down very well. The Experimentals were expected to become geniuses, super human defenders of the Truth; they weren't engineered to become a bunch of idealistic activists nor mixed-up kids.

Despite the generous funding and the academic credentials of the committee members, the experiment mostly backfired. Something had gone terribly wrong: of the 8 scientifically engineered and carefully indoctrinated creatures, only 2 graduated, Maxim and a female co-Experimental, Mixam.

Two other mates became irreversibly insane, 2 developed homicidal inclinations, another 2 dropped out of the experiment at age 20 (it was allowed to do so pending a permission granted by the UP) and became homeless vagrant backpackers wandering throughout the Solar System with no apparent purpose.

Maxim and the female mate whose full name was

Mixam1111AAA graduated with honors at a Committee Commencement Ceremony that took place in 2060, Earth Calendar.

Mixam was actually a very attractive woman with a snub nose, raven hair, violet eyes, a statuesque body and delicate facial features. Unfortunately, she turned out to become a ruthless, unbearably greedy and sadistic creature. Maxim and Mixam never met again, the last he heard from her was that she was running an iridium mine operated by androids on Pluto. She exploited the robots mercilessly 24 by 7 until the poor things either exploded or melted down. To aggravate things for the robots there was very little android labor protection on Pluto.

Maxim had always craved to get to know planet Earth. He was tired of living on the Moon, where at least half of the population consisted of artificial intelligence creatures of all sorts and the other half of mostly unfriendly people who thought they were exceptional just because they lived on the Moon. He'd heard wonderful things about Earth despite all the degradation the Blue Planet's ecosystem had suffered including the huge islands of plastic debris floating on the oceans.

What Maxim enjoyed above all was Earth's atmosphere. Since he was essentially a member of the human species he could move around the planet's continents breathing air in the open. On Earth he didn't have to be confined to geodesic domes with artificial suns and didn't need to wear space suits as he did when he went out of the atmosphere-controlled domes on the Moon or on Mars.

One fine lunar day Maxim decided to move to Earth. He needed find a sunny place where people could breathe fresh air naturally and dress light at least most of the time. After roaming the Blue Planet for a few years, occasionally performing technical work for astonished bosses who had never seen anyone with such unbelievable mathematical skills, Maxim ended up in a place where people dressed very scantily indeed, at least in summertime. He loved *that*.

It took a few months until he adapted to the high temperatures: in summertime it got so hot between 9am and 5 pm that he couldn't stay outdoors for more than an hour. At least, there was plenty of air conditioned public spaces at the Beach Park in front of the hotel he was staying at, the Copa Moon. Also, one (like him, with his Moon-pale skin) couldn't stay under the Sun for more than 30 minutes or would risk becoming a red lobster (this is merely a metaphor, real lobsters had become extinct many years before, paying a heavy price for tasting so good). On the other hand, there was plenty of shade in Copacabana's Beach Park, to which he adapted gradually and learned to enjoy. It was located in Copacabana district, a seaside neighborhood located in the megalopolis named Riosp.

Maxim was sitting inside a glass enclosed bar named The Copa Beach Club. It was located by the shoreline, close to the green and blue waters; the bar catered mostly to foreign tourist who enjoyed the fine views and the air conditioning, kept at a comfortable 20 ° Centigrade while outside the temperature was reaching 42°.

Maxim was sipping the inevitable *caipirinha* when he noticed a celestial human body passing by just in front of him, between the Beach Club and the water. Having become used to employ quantitative analysis as part of his daily life, Maxim immediately evaluated at above 99% the probability of that heavenly body being that of a human female. In itself, that was nothing unusual considering he was on a beach.

However, there was something singular about her; it was the way she moved. She seemed to be almost floating in the air, bouncing gently her body sidewise or so he thought. She moved with exceptional demeanor and grace. He couldn't see her face very well, but he didn't have to. He felt an unprecedented gravitational, irresistible magnetic attraction for that creature who was apparently a human female.

Partly influenced by the hot weather's effect over the rational spheres of his mind and partly by an unexplainable beastly primeval pull, Maxim stood up and for the first time in his life he couldn't quite process rationally what was going on with him; no quantitative analysis could account for his behavior. His reasoning had melted down almost completely as he walked straight ahead towards that strange object of his desire.

What he didn't and couldn't have known was that Experimentals had been prevented from feeling any kind of sexual desire throughout their entire lives. The Committee didn't want 4 healthy young super females and 4 healthy young super males to feel any kind of sexual urge that could disturb the concentration Experimentals needed to have in order to endure the speed-learning process; they had decided so.

Therefore, all Experimentals had been secretly "nourished" with a highly effective libido inhibitor substance disguised as vitamin C. The Committee relentlessly insisted that all vital energy had to be used to build up scientific knowledge accumulation and not be wasted in carnal activities. This was a very well-kept secret.

Every time Experimentals went on entertainment binges as hard-earned rewards for outstanding scholastic performance, they noticed that human beings, unlike the androids, did feel something that was hard to understand when they got together. And it wasn't merely friendship, a feeling that was also practically unknown to the Experimentals. It seemed to be some kind of momentary hyper-excitement, perhaps a side effect of the powerful animal attraction that could potentially be felt between opposite genders and, at times, among humans from the same gender. Funny humans, Experimentals would confide to themselves.

Sexual attraction was a strictly banned topic of conversation among the Experimentals. Whenever they expressed any degree of curiosity on the subject, they were cut short and assured by their instructors that being a higher form of human species they were too detached from the lower, more primitive human categories. That they stood at a much higher level, well above other humans on the scale of Darwinian evolution. Therefore, "no more talk about sex, please"...

However, after graduation the former Experimentals weren't taking the libido-inhibiting substances any longer. Therefore, most of them began to feel those ancestral, animal urges once they moved on with their lives. Such was the case with Maxim.

Maxim walked straight toward that dream-like female and as she moved further away, he banged his head straight into the glass that enclosed the bar; he dropped his *caipirinha* on the floor, slipped on the ice cubes and almost fell down too. He just didn't get seriously hurt due to the fact that the material the transparent wall was made of was not really glass, but a semi soft version of transparent CM^3.

Finding, haphazardly, his way out of the bar, he walked in a hurry after the female floating marvel. Finally reaching her, and using the Brazilian Portuguese language skills he had acquired as an Experimental, he tried to say something, but he just couldn't find the appropriate words. Maxim made a supreme effort to say anything and, at the same time, to keep his voice under control so he wouldn't frighten the young female:

PLEASE STOP!

3   CM – Condensed Matter

Bruna was entirely caught by surprise. She turned around, touched gently her left ear's lobe and turned off something. She had actually been listening to The Red Dusters, a Martian metallic rock band in a-lobe implanted micro system.

Bruna raised her sunglasses and stared at him with her yellow-brown opal eyes. The drop dead look she gave him almost completed the job that the transparent CM walls hadn´t been able to do: he almost got knocked down to the sandy park surface.

What? – asked Bruna, somewhat alarmed.

The number of misfits, erratic people of all ages and nutty guys and girls that one could notice on the streets had increased a lot in the past few years. It seemed as if all humankind was becoming gradually plain crazy lately. But that pale male didn't look threatening at all. Bruna quickly noticed that he was a handsome male, even though the very pale color of his skin didn't exactly enhance his good looks.

– Stop for a moment! – shouted Maxim.

– What's the matter with you?

– Excuse me, but I need to ask you a question?

– Oh, no! You're an exoteric cult solicitor!

– No, not at all!

– So what do you want?

– I just want to ask you a question!

– Hmm?

– Are you a human female?

– Whaaat? Have you jumped off a spaceship?

– Mmm, actually I just have. I mean, no. I mean, yeah, I'm from the Moon, but I've been around the Beach Park for some time.

That wasn't something very unusual. The Beach Park was crowded with Moony tourists. One could tell them by their paper white skins, huge *sombrero* hats and thick dark sunglasses.

– And why did you come running after me?

– I don't know. I'm so sorry.

– What do you mean, you don't know?

– I can't think of a reason I acted in this way. I never did something like this before. I usually precede all my actions with a previous quantitative analysis check!

– Gee, you're weird, Moonies are weird… Anyway, who are you, space creature?

– I'm sorry. I guess I should have introduced myself. I'm Maxim 3131ZX.

Maxim extended his right hand's index finger to her, a formal way of greeting someone who you had just become acquainted with. She extended her left hand's index finger and touched his (Bruna was mostly left handed, even though she also had ambidextrous abilities).

– I'm Bruna1431KL and yes, I'm a human female – she replied with an ironic smirk.

– I feel like an idiot, I'm so sorry. I've lived all my life mostly surrounded by female robots. I'm very glad to meet a human female. You look… natural.

– Oh, really?

– And you have hair! Is your hair natural?

– Gee, Mr. Spaceman, I'm afraid I need to go…

– Oh, please don't! My implanted oracle is signaling that today is a day of great importance in my life. It tells me that I must insist that you stay with me for some time, that I must invite you for a drink just as an excuse to spend more time with you.

– Mr. Spaceman, my intuition tells me I must go.

– Uh, may I invite you for a drink? We can go to a bar with dangerous invisible walls.

– You're inviting me to an invisible bar…

– Kind of, it has invisible walls; maybe we can go for a *caipirinha*. You just have to be careful with the invisible walls.

The notion of sipping a *caipirinha*, a drink that was consumed almost exclusively by (first-time) tourists in Rio sounded gross and ridiculous.

Bruna began to signal that she was about to take-off from the scene of the weird encounter. Maxim almost panicked but, realizing that his performance had been less than impressive, he tried to restrain himself in order not to cause an even more ludicrous impression.

Alright, would you mind leaving me your *wise com* number and password?

Let's do it the other way around. Give me your *wise com* protocols.

Alright, thank you, please give me a call.

I haven't made up my mind yet. I don't know if you're a burned out android, a Moony nut or just a spaceman lost on Earth.

Don't worry. I'm not as bad as I seem to be, not as crazy. And I guess I'm 100% human.

Oh, what a relief.

Please call me.

See you later, Spaceman.

Please call.

That night, for the first time in his life, Maxim had wet dreams as he slept profoundly.

***

Bruna had to admit that Maxim was, at least, a perfect gentleman with her; actually, too perfect, too much of a gentleman. Maxim never raised his voice at her and frequently pampered Bruna with all kinds of exquisite gifts.

Bruna liked the gentlemanlike side of Maxim's personality; she'd grown used to being treated as someone special. She had been born the old fashioned way, in a maternity, from male and female human parents who even loved each other.

Little Bruna turned out to be a very smart girl from a very early age; she had played with all kinds of smart educational toys, puzzles, and was able to build alone simple multifunctional toy robots at age 5.

She was her daddy's little princess and he always fulfilled all her wishes and whims. Bruna's mother also gave her love and dedication, but demanded from her the highest scholastic performing standards; Bruna had to be at least among the top students in her age group. And she was educated at some of the finest schools and colleges on the planet, expensive institutions that almost led her devoted parents to bankruptcy.

Many years later, after Bruna (yes, she *did call him* after a couple of days and they did eventually start dating) and Maxim had become *civil cohabitants*, the latter never forgot to bring Bruna her favorite fragrance every time he returned from a journey to Mars: a flask of *Fleur de Mars*, extracted from rare green truffles discovered in the Red Planet beneath the ice caps. An ounce of the perfume would go for over 6000 *astrodollars* in any of that planet's duty-free shops.

Another favorite with Bruna was that planetary splurge among women (and many males, as well), the much sought after creamy miracle, Perenial27. It was scientifically proven to halt and freeze the facial aging process. Maxim was not impressed with the price tag of these items; he would foot the bill without blinking. The sky was the limit when it came to please his passionate Bruna. And he meant the interplanetary sky.

She gave him credit for his openhandedness and conceded her *civil cohabitant* did have a few strong points. However, she didn't just want him to behave nicely or generously with her: she'd love to see him get furious, to yell at her. Even to raise his voice a bit at her would have been alright. Instead, his rationality and frosty politeness were disconcerting. Maxim's eyes looked like those of a dead fish in the market. His gesturing was minimal, his reactions, predictable. The man was a data processing cold-logic machine. Maybe that's why he got selected as a spaceship pilot in the first place.

Bruna would chill at the notion that Maxim might be, in fact, an *androhybrid creature*, part human and part android. He wouldn't be the only one in those *worlds*. In his generation, scientists had begun to develop "enhanced" human beings through genetic engineering and organ replacement. Besides, *androchemistry* had advanced tremendously with the discovery of acids capable of stimulating brain, nerves and muscles.

Bruna increasing levels of anxiety with Maxim's usually unemotional behavior made her seek professional help. She began to look for a psychotherapist. It took a long time before Bruna felt comfortable with one. Finally, she found a female therapist, Dr. Rafaela Froid, who was able to tranquilize Bruna a bit by revealing that Maxim's conduct was quite standard for those days. Maxim was a top performer, had outstanding mathematical abilities and his behavior was quite coherent with his overall profile. After all, he was not a poet; he was an astronaut, and one of the best.

Bruna herself was evaluated and diagnosed as a *"Functional Contempogyneco Irritabilis"* – *FCI G22*. This evaluation was done in accordance with the *Planetary Diagnostic and Statistical Manual, PDSM 1*(that superseded the US-compiled manual DSM 8). To Dr. Froid, this was not an infrequent category for a female in that era of high expectations, resulting frustrations and arguably complete gender equality. To aggravate things, she was also a wife in love with her husband or rather, in 2065 talk, a human female with a high level of empathy and tolerance for her *civil cohabitant.*

Despite Dr. Froid's reassurances, it seems that Bruna

had a point. Maxim *was* peculiar; actually, downright complicated. His eating habits often included tofu salad with quinoa seeds, which in itself was a reasonable choice for a healthy meal. There were billions of conscientious human beings who had opted for vegan and natural foods. However, his salad *had* to include hydroponic algae from Venus on the side. Maxim had adhered to the latest trend in human dieting; he was a *Vevegan,* those who added produce from Venus to their vegan meals. But these Venus foods weren't always readily available. Also, he drank natural spring water, a very costly beverage in a semi-arid planet, and also, either chlorophyll juice or hibiscus flower water.

Bruna, instead, was an accomplished omnivore. She loved grilled beefsteaks, barbecued prawns, and occasionally, something more exotic like carnivore-flower *capeletti* from planet Venus, that she leaned to enjoy by her contact with Maxim. She also had a liking for complicated drinks such as *Nin Tchau Dark,* a mix of vodka, gin, bitter, crème de cassis, champagne brut, Amazon rainforest açaí berry, dry ice, and an egg white. It all came in a tall glass complete with a large purple swizzle stick made to resemble a giant lollipop with a smiling half a moon on the top. One of her favorite wines was a Brazilian *Taste-Alike* Pinot Noir Burgundy from the High Central Plateau which had won the first prize at the Shanghai Wine Expo 2059.

For Maxim, the definition of great living was (when he wasn't away piloting to and from Mars) to remain secluded in his *fun studio* within the SLU (*Smart Living Unit*) he shared with Bruna. The SLU was an intelligent self-cleaning flat where all household appliances interacted with the robots in charge of all different aspects of house planning and housekeeping.

Despite their differences, which at times seemed irreconcilable, Bruna was willing to invest her emotional fragility and precious time in Maxim. She thought he was physically attractive and had a brilliant mind, even though his emotional intelligence left much to be desired. But he had achieved universal professional recognition and that counted a lot in 2065.

Three ULATAM pilots had been selected (among 120 candidates from the entire world) to conduct the Embra-Boeing Interplanetary Super XL300 Spaceship, assembled in São José dos Campos, São Paulo, Brazil. It now regularly linked Tom Jobim Spaceport with Mars. Maxim now belonged to the elite of terrestrial pilots.

Three

STATISTICS REVEALED THAT IN 2065 only 30% of the population of Riosp lived in some kind of family arrangement. Almost 70% lived alone, albeit surrounded by a vast array of digital paraphernalia and an occasional domestic android.

In strictly legal terms, marriage was now called *Civil Cohabitation* and could be dissolved at any given moment by either of the cohabitants involved without consulting the other spouse. All one needed to do was to enter the site of the Ministry of Virtual Justice, digit the appropriate password and delete the relationship. In the "reason for divorce" entry, it was enough to digit ETOL4 (Empathy and Tolerance level 4). ETOL4 was a valid justification for divorce. And send a copy to your spouse.

Bruna felt empathy with and tolerated her *cohabitant* at a safe level of ETOL8 (Empathy and Tolerance level 8). That was regarded as quite high on the scale from 1 to 10 which had replaced, for all legal effects, any notion of love and hatred. These feelings had been officially abolished thanks to the efforts of well-intentioned activists who were disturbed by human inequality in its capacity to love and hate. The spirit of these newly-adopted concepts had been incorporated into existing legislation as constitutional amendments. They had been duly approved by the DDD (as we've learned, this was the Digital Direct Democracy adopted by the nation). At least human emotions hadn't been criminalized, but much controversy ensued.

ETOL8 was considered a very high level of affection in this narcissistic, hedonistic world of 2065, where egos competed fiercely. Almost everybody in *these worlds* full of mirrors and ephemeral celebrities were convinced they had the right to feel unique and exceptional. Everyone was a unique and exceptional individual.

Humans were free to behave as they pleased as long as they didn't break the law. That is to say, as long as they weren't caught by the almighty ULATAM Trilateral Police. This powerful organization had adopted a strict policy of Online Zero Tolerance (OZT).

In order to enforce this policy, over 12 million microscopic cameras were installed everywhere in the Continent. More specifically, in all avenues, streets, alleys, corners, bridges, roads, squares and parks, beaches, stores, restaurants, theaters, show halls, stadiums, elevators and vehicles; in hospitals, clinics and labs; in offices, police precincts, factories and industrial plants. Despite much opposition, they were even installed in all public and even in some private toilets. Not to speak of more obvious locations, such as subways, railway stations, airports and spaceports. That is to say, on every single spot in the Continent.

The images the cameras sent in were monitored and processed by specialized, highly advanced androids. Besides, all digital and telecom exchanges were permanently monitored by the Trilateral.

Many libertarians were unhappy with this unconditional interference in people's private lives, but most were willing to give up their individual rights in exchange for more security; and not only in ULATAM.

This new supranational force had substituted all police forces and public-safety corporations in Latin America.

It was co-headquartered in three locations: Santiago de Chile, The Hague (The Netherlands) and Geneva (Switzerland), hence its name. In this latter location, the auditing of all Trilateral's activities was conducted online. Santiago had been selected as another co-headquarters because the Carabineros de Chile was reputed to be the most incorruptible police force in Latin America.

Understandably, all other police forces in the Continent became desperately jealous and were up in arms. They demonstrated their discontent publicly and many even went on strike. They caused a scandal of Continental dimensions and many appealed to the individual nation's sense of patriotism. They alleged breaches of the national sovereignty of each of ULATAM's units. Some police corporations even attempted to stage rebellions and regional coups but to no avail. At the end of the day, in 2050, they had to submit to popular will, frustrated by their police forces' ineptitude, indifference and dismal lack of commitment to society.

The people of Latin America went to the streets to demand immediate solutions: it was impossible to tackle widespread criminality while a corrupt culture and shady practices prevailed in practically all areas of public security throughout the Continent.

People were sick and tired of "special operations" ineffective policies. They couldn't stand any longer those sporadic demonstrations of force, such as calling in temporarily Special Forces during major international events just to leave the population unprotected again as soon as the local authorities bade farewell to the last foreign delegation. This was standard practice adopted in most Latin-American countries just to appease the foreign press and avoid criticism every time an event was staged in one of its notoriously high-crime rate cities. People craved for non-stop, full-time safety.

Citizens began to demand permanent and sustainable public policies and practices. They finally lost their patience with all those idealistic and naïve sociological and philosophical points of view which contended that after a few generations of high-quality public education crime rates would drop gradually. Those viewpoints seemed to ignore the somber side of human nature and the far reaching power of highly organized crime. They also ignored the power of popular outrage.

The public demanded immediate improvement in public security. If necessary, they were willing to appeal directly for the displacement of highly effective Special Forces from the UN and the UP.

The most professionally qualified and idealistic elements among the existing public security corporations, often working for the federal police forces of some nations, were retrained by the Trilateral and integrated in the New Order. Other forces were reassigned as electronic surveillance officers for security-support functions. Others were simply dissolved. And some were even put behind bars.

ULATAM's most potentially dangerous criminals were sent for incarceration in Chile, a nation-member of the ULATAM Confederation. Chile made huge profits playing the role of Continental jail keeper. Unlike the frequent rebellions, in-prison assassinations and mass escapes that occurred in most of the penitentiaries in the rest of Latin America, even at the so-called "high security" ones, an inmate hardly ever escaped from a Chilean OZT Trilateral Correctional Unit.

Rogue humanoids, extremely dangerous creatures, were outlawed according to international conventions, but were often assembled in rogue labs of the Failed States of the World and shipped in a clandestine way to ULATAM. Now, when captured, they were sent to specialized penitentiaries in The Netherlands, by now an Autonomous

State in the European Federation. This was standard procedure since their mere elimination had been prohibited by interplanetary treaties as their quasi human status was the object of widespread controversy. In fact, many of these rogue humanoids were even admired by many: their capacity to commit evil deeds was as refined as that of the most devilish human beings.

With OZT policies and other severe measures adopted, crime and corruption rates in all sectors of public security had been reduced, in most of ULATAM, to Western European levels. An extraordinary achievement, widely publicized in every sort of media: VIVA OZT, VIVA ULATAM!

In 2065, as we've seen, it was common belief that all human dreams, aspirations and cravings should necessarily come true at once. Everyone wanted to shine, to receive recognition and applause, to enjoy life without restrictions and to seek pleasure non-stop. *Ultra hedonism* was in. Everybody felt entitled to become a *nano celebrity* for at least 15 seconds. Even Andy Warhol would have been surprised had he lived for another one hundred years.

The Human Happiness Index (HHI), a self-perception gage of how happy people felt, was measured on a scale of 0 to 10. It was regarded as satisfactory to be at level 7.

Happiness was defined as the sum of accomplishments of an individual's narcissistic dreams. Each individual was led to believe that he or she was unique and exceptional, just as some nations had done in the past. But now what mattered was to become a Solar-Systemic, not merely an international, celebrity.

Meanwhile, the Blue Planet's population had increased to over 11 billion; the average annual temperature of the planet had increased by 5 degrees Celsius over the past 100 years, its oceans were slowly rising and its soil was drying up gradually. The major concern was whether there would be sufficient physical space and resources to accommodate not only the huge planetary population, but also such widespread narcissism (since narcissistic people tend to occupy more space and consume more goods than ordinary fellows) on a global scale.

Confronted with such harsh realities, a Solar System Conference, under the auspices of the UN and the UP (United Planets Organization) was being held in the latter's Headquarters, on the Moon's Sea of Tranquility area.

UP's Headquarters had already been built right in the epicenter of New Earth/ Terra Nova (NETN) City. It was built inside a giant dome measuring 2 kilometers in diameter that was linked to multiple other domes of the same size.

NETN (pronounced *Net'n*) was a rather wild and dissolute city, overcrowded with those colossal casinos and multiple sleazy leisure centers.

Paradoxically, it was run very efficiently by a multi-planetary consortium and had an interplanetary population of about 50,000 inhabitants, without counting the androids.

All of NETN's dwellers lived in neighborhoods planned and built inside gigantic geodesic domes that were connected to each other. NETN was, in reality, a cluster of interconnected giant domes.

Humans couldn't survive outside the acclimatized and gravity neutralized domes without space suits. They could and did get out of the domes, always in guided groups, when they felt like. But all humans and most humanoids were expected to live inside the domes. Some of the domes' diameters (containing big casinos and theme parks) even reached as far as 6 kilometers.

The main intention of the Solar System Conference was to discuss, plan and raise funding for the planned emigration of masses of Earthlings to other planets and, eventually, to other Galaxies, in spite of all difficulties and hazards.

Discussions had been ongoing for 10 years and little progress had been made. One of the topics that had become a stumbling block among participants was over the right of Earth's Federations and Confederations to export their predatory and environmentally-unfriendly model of "development" to other planets and virtually ruin their ecosystems just as they did with Earth´s. Did humans have the right to export their economic model, their lifestyle, and their narcissistic civilization to other planets and galaxies?

***

Psychotherapy offices were packed, either with high income private patients or with those who benefitted from Social Happiness Programs (SHP) adopted by many nations.

Bruna was perfectly at ease in that world ruled under the sign of Narcissus and Ego. In regard to pleasure, life enjoyment and impatience to accomplish her goals, Bruna, now 32 years old, was a perfect example of her generation, the YYZZ. All their wishes had to come true immediately.

At times Bruna, while asleep, wore her US-made *Dreamtime Pillow Mask*, in which you could program and record your dreams, deleting the nightmares. It included a number of screenplay and ending options. This gave consumers the illusion of being movie directors while they slept. And after *Pillow Mask* users woke up, they could watch their dreams again and again.

The alpha numeric tag 1431KL attached to Bruna's name was some sort of exclusive personal patent that had become universally adopted by those who wished to look special and could afford it. It gave its title holder the right to be the legal owner of that particular identification in the whole Solar System. All one needed to do was to apply and pay annual fees to the UN and to the UP Human Patent Office. It also gave the bearer the right to wear a titanium plate collar with the identification engraved on it.

But there was something about Bruna that was not typical of her age at all. Actually, in strictly emotional terms Bruna was quite untypical: she wanted to be loved and desired! Now, *that* was something odd in the opinion of most of her friends and acquaintances.

Bruna also had a hard time in suppressing emotions. She wept tearfully when sad or displeased. Everyone was amazed to witness those real liquid tears, an unusual occurrence at a time when almost all adult-age people on the planet had run out of tears. Humankind's tears had simply dried up.

And yet Bruna's most extravagant feature was her willingness to procreate with Maxim and become an old-fashioned mom.

She had been taking her pill for three months. It wasn't that old-time, conventional birth-control pill. Instead, it was a pink Derepblo capsule that rendered females fertile again and therefore, apt for reproduction.

When Bruna had reached puberty, following her first menstrual period she, as many females of her generation (in most Western societies), was submitted to a minimally invasive procedure named Repblo (reproductive blockade).This procedure temporarily halted women's capacity to reproduce. There was no need of intra uterine devices and it was risk free. It was considered a major scientific breakthrough aimed at giving women the full mastery of her right to orgasm without fearing its consequences. Women were now free to enjoy their orgasmic gift from nature, without guilt or worries of any kind, and without becoming infertile.

Furthermore, with the end of the need to interrupt any undesirable pregnancy with an abortion, the Vatican had approved the Repblo procedure at the 2055 Council of Las Vegas, under the papacy of His Holiness, Pope Pop the Second. The decisive argument of the Pro-Female Orgasm Cool Bishops' Association, was that there was no risk of pregnancy since the female egg cells were safely blocked. No undesired new life would risk having to be interrupted. And Derepblo, the new pill, just restored to women their reproductive capability. After the third dosage, they became as fertile as they had been at the onset of their puberty.

For Bruna, the craving to have a child was visceral, something primeval. She couldn't even disclose the matter to most of her real life friends. For them, maternity was simply out of question. It was regarded as a mere nuisance, a hindrance to the fulfillment of a narcissistic lifestyle.

An independent production, without any legal bond with a semen donor through a sperm bank was another option. However, females were so demanding about the characteristics of the baby to be produced that finding the perfect match was nearly impossible. They aspired to have babies that were, at the same time beautiful, with great potential to become famous and with privileged genes that would yield geniuses. It was all very complicated.

With the widespread use of gene boosters and body enhancers, one could finally project an alpha human. The matter, however, caused so much controversy among members of the UN and the UP that a temporary ban on human enhancement and genetic engineering was agreed upon, to the bitter disappointment of trendy *baby designers*. These were up in arms: their tantrums echoed throughout the Galaxy.

An informal male donor, be it a friend or an acquaintance, was hard to find due to the legal responsibilities the act entailed. Even harder was a biological father who also happened to be a civil cohabitant. Maxim, as most humans from his generation, was totally opposed to the idea of having children. He wouldn't even discuss the matter. But Bruna was equally persistent.

Bruna was a certified Moon real estate broker dealing with exclusive private condos built on the lunar surface. (" – Oh dear, take a look at the beautiful Earth we're having tonight!" – was the standard pitch). They were sold with title deeds issued by the UP plus a UN disclaimer. But lunar real estate was not for anyone, the asking price for a basic loft began at 220 million *astrodollars,* a respectable amount of money.

Four

— *NIN HAO!* — **GREETED BRUNA** when she finally saw Maxim3131XZ leaving the *space tunnel.*

— *Nin hao*, Bruna, replied Maxim, while kissing her lips in a dry and almost mechanical fashion. It was hardly the passionate love kiss she dreamed about, but that's the way it was with Maxim. And a dry kiss was better than no kiss at all.

In 2065 almost all humans greeted each other using the expression *nin hao*, in Mandarin Chinese. After all, China's influence in the planet wasn't only economic, it had wide cultural implications. *Nin hao* had become a universal buzz word. And to say goodbye, the hybrid Mandarin-Italian expression *nin ciao* (pronounced *nin-tchao*) was also widely employed. Even the Chinese adopted the hybrid term after their billionth (yes, one billionth!) tourist had visited Italy. The Chinese went nuts with Italy, with all those monuments and statues. Consortiums of Chinese billionaires even offered to purchase and retrofit the Coliseum of Rome. Yes, to restore it exactly as it stood in the days of the Caesars, in marble and all. Some businesses even considered re-enacting gladiatorial fights with androids. The Chinese would obviously foot the bill. They offered an undisclosed but presumably astronomical amount of money, enough to feed every Italian with a daily pizza for one hundred years! The Italians replied that *that* was neither a good archaeological nor dietary practice. Anyway, *nin ciao* remained as a fine, if awkward, blending of East and West in a highly integrated planetary era.

The media went wild about the quick kiss the astronaut gave the lunar real estate broker. Within a few seconds that dry and dull kiss was edited and enhanced a bit and then broadcasted to the confines of the Solar System. Maxim and Bruna had become *nanocelebrities* for 15 seconds.

Both left TJSP's terminal 10 in a hurry, leaving behind a horde of reporters. These worked as free-lancers for all sorts of media. They now tackled and tumbled each other to the floor and shouted wildly trying to grab the attention and perhaps a few words from the tight-lipped mouth of the *nano celebrity* pilot who was returning from planet Mars. But Maxim had nothing to declare.

Some of the reporters worked for an important news-paper, The Galaxy, which printed a paper-version daily. It was, in fact, printed in LED paper, *photo* and *psycho sensitive,* interactive and online. It was a totally customized paper, supplying the reader with the news compatible with his or her preference. It was aligned with one's ideology and even lifestyle. The Galaxy didn't want dissatisfied readers. There was also a Happy News-only version, the Happy Life Journal, for those who were sick and tired of all of the world's sorrows and had decided to read only joyful and funny stories.

The couple finally got into Bruna's vehicle. Maxim didn't notice the new flag depicted on the side panels of the car. With Bruna in the driver's seat (Maxim had had enough of driving), they rushed home. Restless and anxious as ever, Bruna ascended to the highest level allowed by Urban Air Traffic Control, 6000 ft., at 470 km an hour, a very expensive elliptical maneuver that would cost her

9000 NR$ in toll fees. She docked the vehicle at one of the 12 vehicle parking lots assigned to her unit at the Blue Water Towers condo in exactly 2 minutes and 14 seconds.

This was a most exclusive address, located at the end of Copacabana Beach Park. The towers were built at the site where in the past Fort Copacabana had existed. The famous beach and sidewalk had become enlarged fourfold, expanding into the Ocean. Thus, millions of people could now sunbathe with more comfort on weekends, at public parties and on those New Year's Eve monumental ceremonies.

The 18 towers that projected themselves for a kilometer into the sea had been built by a Chinese-Brazilian engineering consortium strictly within the maximum height limit of 120 stories, not including the 20 floors used for garage facilities.

The couple lived on the 110th. floor, apartment 11001. The view was astonishing. From the balcony one could easily notice the curvature of the planet on the horizon. Most of the tower walls were made of translucent *neo titanium*.

Initially, the Brazilian Army objected to the plan, but the Chinese made an offer of NR$ 3 trillion to be utilized for the re-fitting the Armed Forces. These had been all but neglected for the past 70 years by consecutive administrations and were in pitiful condition. Besides, the site had no strategic value.

After extensive negotiations, it was also agreed, for an additional NR$ 2 trillion, to include the purchase of a military reservation at the other end of Copacabana, for the construction of another condo featuring 18 mega towers. In 2065, to maintain the Armed Forces on a State of Immediate Response in strategic partnership with ULATAM brought along a considerable price tag. All decisions had been made with the approval of Digital Democracy.

The developers decided to keep the giant 1914

Krupp-made German guns of Fort Copacabana inside the Blue Water Towers playground, duly de-activated, to entertain the kids.

The very moment they set foot on the flat, Bruna began to feel intense waves of sexual desire building up in her body. She had de-activated the couple's three domestic robots so they wouldn't be watching their bosses while they coupled. Humanoids, not having been programmed by the manufacturers to feel any sexual desire whatsoever, and therefore suffering from an absolute absence of libido, were unable to have sexual intercourse. On the other hand, they loved peeking in disguise at their master's sexual activities. They were incorrigible *voyeurs*.

However, to Bruna's disappointment, Maxim threw his voyage handbag on the living rooms' floor and hurried up to his *fun studio*. He directed his right hand's pointing finger towards his 2000 square feet *wall screen*. It began broadcasting a soccer game directly from the Moon Soccer Dome. It was, in fact, a LGS, *Low Gravity Soccer* game, developed by the Americans, featuring a 600 feet long (and 300 ft. wide) field, with 100 feet-high jumping and spectacular 400 feet soccer ball kicks. The game was being played between the European LGS Federation League's team and ULATAM's Continental LGS League team. It was estimated that total attendance throughout the Solar System would reach 8 billion. Everybody was supposed to watch the game. Everybody but Bruna, she had other plans.

Bruna jumped ahead right away and pointed her thumb at the *wall screen*, turning off the giant entertainment system.

– Sh###t! – Keep this damn screen switched off, today I want to *couple* with you!

– Oh, Bruna dear, don't get annoyed but my *bio pulsar* watch is warning me that I'm 18 Earth hours and 42 Earth minutes behind both in terms of *space lag* and in terms of my own *point zero bio clock*. I can't couple under these un-favorable conditions.

– *Mega shits10!* I don't care what these *pulsars* and *bio clocks* tell! I'm already tired of locking myself up inside my *orgasbord capsule* every time I'm in heat. I demand to couple with you right know!

– Sorry, Bruna dear, not today.

– But if I don't couple with you today I'll get frustrated!

– Sorry, Bruna dear, but it just won't happen today.

– But you know that I just can't cope with frustration!

– Nobody can, Bruna dear, nobody can.

– Since I decided to get pregnant and began to take the pill you just won't couple with me anymore! *Shiiii#$%!!!*

– And you don't need to keep shouting *sh&&%%!* and *fu%$##*. It's not sexy, I think it's vulgar and I get bored.

– Every man in this city would do anything to *couple* with me! But you are the man I want! I just want to *couple* with you!

– Thanks for the compliment. It seems that your *shrink* has done a tremendous job on your self-esteem. But I won't discuss this matter for the next 48, perhaps 72 hours. I travelled too many light-years to get home and have to put up with an argument like this. I know your frustration might bring about unhappy consequences to our relationship. But today I don't feel like engaging in an argument with you just as I don't feel like having sexual intercourse with you. I'm exhausted and I'm not even completely re-adapted to Earth's atmosphere. So please excuse me.

– I get your point, Maxim, but I'm at the height of my fertile period and I feel... very ... *horny* today.

– I'd rather not listen to any further detail. This is becoming an embarrassment to both of us. Please, I need to go...

– Take a look at my *wrist pulsar*, it shows that my chances of getting pregnant would be 96,25%! – screamed Bruna.

– And my *pulsar* shows that I'm only at 63% of my *stamina vital* optimal level, it won't work. I would need to take an overdose of Bombax – replied Maxim without raising his voice.

– No problem, I'll bring you Bombax right away!

– Not today, Bruna. Not today, I'm afraid – replied Maxim without blinking. Besides, according to the Earth Mars Shuttle Handbook I should still be in the re-adaptation facility at EETJ. And your *pulsar index summary* also shows you are 37.7% out of control at this precise moment. You're getting close to the violent behavior zone. So... please excuse me.

Bruna stared at her mate. She couldn't believe it! She couldn't accept as real what had just happened, that surrealistic exchange of words and that outburst of emotions on her part. She felt exposed, vulnerable, humiliated, but she held back her tears. He didn't deserve to see her sobbing.

On the other hand, Maxim didn't seem to be disturbed at all. His dead fish facial expression was intact. It was all truly scary... Those eyes, how weird they were.... Their color and tonality varied according to his state of mind. Now, they were grayish and glossy.

Bruna concluded there was nothing else she could do about her *coupling* with Maxim. She wouldn't beg for sex. That was beneath her sense of self-esteem, even in moment of fragility like that one. She wouldn't do that for any man in the Galaxy, not even for Maxim.

She walked away in fury heading for her own *fun studio,* but first she stepped into her anti-frustration closet, a mid-sized self-cleaning room projected by a Japanese firm, Banzai Inc. After dressing her light titanium armor and equipped with a good old-fashioned baseball bat, Bruna began smashing second-hand chinaware, fake classical Greek vases, unwanted vintage furniture, mirrors, and then concentrated her frustration on a Maxim look – alike wax figure dressed in an astronaut's spacesuit. Bruna spent 30 minutes smashing the vases, statues, mirrors, the astronaut dummy. As the room was self-cleaning she just walked out of the place. In another 15 minutes all smashed pieces would have been replaced and the room would be tidy and neat, thanks to the cleaning robots. The place would be ready for yet another of Bruna's tantrums.

After destroying everything she possibly could and feeling more relieved, she got into her Danish-designed *Orgasbord capsule*. It was actually manufactured under license in United Korea. She regulated the intensity of the orgasm she desired to have at level 7.5 with duration of 8 minutes and pressed *start*.

Eight minutes later Bruna got off the capsule feeling relaxed and temporarily happy. She stepped inside Maxim's *fun studio* to take a look at him. He was sleeping like a baby on his *futon*, in fetal position. He was nearly sucking his thumb.

Bruna sighed in disgust. She went to her home office craving to sell a few more housing units in the Sea of Tranquility before she went to bed. She launched the ad into cyberspace:

FUN STUDIOS ON THE MOON GO ON SALE!
50 sq. meter-units (about 500 sq.ft.) for only 200 million alpha dollars.
A COSMIC KILLING!

The pitch worked and within half an hour she sold 32 units to customers throughout the Solar System.

Relaxed and relieved, she went to bed in her own *fun studio* without the need of any chemical aid whatsoever, something unusual in those *mega frantic* days.

While she was beginning to fall asleep, Bruna kept reflecting about how on Earth she would get pregnant from

Maxim. However, deep inside she felt self-confident. Her last thought before she finally dozed off was:

– I'm gonna get exactly what I want, by all means, or my name isn't Bruna1431KL! Bruna kicks ass!

Five

ONE OF THE MOST CONTROVERSIAL TOPICS of discussion in those days was in regard to the legal status of domestic robots. Even at close distance, they looked like real human beings. Should they enjoy legal protection? Should they be allowed to form an association or perhaps a trade union? Some were already shouting:

– "Humanoids of the Solar System, unite!"

In the business environment, things were not less confusing. Should humanoids (*) be bought and sold just like any other merchandize? Could they change ownership? Should there be a secondary market for second-hand humanoids? It was happening already.

With the improvements in artificial skin manufacturing and facial plastic surgery, not to speak of the remarkable advancements in the science of artificial intelligence, the similarity between humanoids and human beings had become so astounding that the makers had to imprint their trademarks and logos inside the irises and on the fingerprints of their products. This would allow consumers to tell humans from machines.

*1 – Humanoid is an all-inclusive expression that includes both androids and gynoids. Android is a robot with male appearance and characteristics while gynoid is a robot with female features.

The looks, the perfect pronunciation of words in many languages, the realistic demeanor of their gestures, the ability to do all the house work perfectly well and without complaining about life, were truly amazing.

Some were even able to sing the classical repertoire. Some gynoid sopranos and android tenors had become universal celebrities, although critics maintained their voices were too metallic. For those with less harmonious preferences, there were even all-humanoid heavy metal rock bands, with some of their members writing their own songs.

Most robots were projected and developed in Japan. Some were manufactured in United Korea under license. Prices ranged greatly depending on the model. More sophisticated humanoids were programmed to execute tasks such as analyzing the cost-benefit of different options and making the most sensible and rational choices when shopping for household goods. Other skills included controlling domestic budgets and supervising other androids. Top of the line humanoids could cost as much as *flexmedia multi-environmental* vehicles.

Humanoid Rights non-governmental organizations (NGO's) were in full activity, struggling for the emancipation of the new serfs that robotic technology had created. The NGO's alleged that even though humanoids didn't have the capacity to feel all the range of emotions humans did, they could already identify, process and evaluate these feelings. And become depressed.

In fact, some more advanced Japanese and Korean models were already able to develop neuroses, to feel *angst* and phobias of different kinds. Some got to the point of needing to be sent, periodically, to their authorized dealers for robotic psychotherapy sessions. A new branch of psychotherapy had come into existence, *Robotherapy*.

Some *humanoids,* under severe stress, acted out completely. In these cases manufacturers were required to have them recalled, have their chips and circuits replaced and have them reprogrammed before they were sent back to their owners. The makers were also liable for any damage their humanoids may have caused.

Paradoxically, all this was happening at a time when the existing civilization was, directly or indirectly, trying to suppress all types of feelings among humans.

In addition, there was little sympathy for those who questioned the egocentric, narcissistic model the planet had adopted and this form of intolerance was expressed both in the academic world and in the social media. It became commonplace to say that this model was "good for the System". Nevertheless, a few writers and other independent minds still disputed this model. They were still allowed to do so, but they were under growing pressure to give in and accept the Established Truth.

Six

LATE FEBRUARY, 2065, EARTH CALENDAR.

At sea level, for the masses enjoying the amenities of Copacabana Beach Park, it was a hot sunny morning. Kids were running around, eating popsicles, playing soccer, volleyball, and refreshing themselves in public showers. The children's pools were closely watched by android life-guards; this special edition of androids was obviously wa-terproof. Children were happily fooling around and run-ning over the grass or the sand. *Riospians* were doing the things adults do on a beach park; most were drinking beer or coconut water. Even though one could see people from all ages having fun in the Beach Park, most individuals seemed to be middle-aged or elderly.

Meanwhile, foreign tourists, mostly elderly as well, were drinking *caipirinhas,* readily available everywhere they'd go. *Caipirinhas* were among the 10 most popular drinks on Earth and all foreigners drank them almost non-stop while in Rio. "If you don't drink *caipirinhas* while in Rio, you're not in Rio".

It was the peak of summer in the Southern Hemisphere and in Rio, on a sunny summer day, temperatures reached, at times, 46º Centigrade (about 115 Fahrenheit) and hu-midity levels were quite high as well. Heat strokes and dehydration were inevitable. But nobody seemed to complain. As long as the Sun was shining out there, as long as the sea water was crystal clear and cold beer was readily available, an atmosphere of bliss prevailed among those scantily dressed and talkative, gregarious people.

Very close to that point, at over a thousand feet high, the whole world was a marvelous blue spectacle and the ocean breeze couldn't be more pleasant. A balmy morning gentle wind was blowing from the ocean; it was fragrant, salty and refreshing.

Bruna, still feeling a bit sleepy and wearing nothing but her purple light Egyptian cotton robe over her tanned skin, greeted her household supervisor with a casual *nin hao*. Tavares2 was a recent-model, state of the art android. He immediately replied:

Nin hao, milady.

Oh, Tavares2, go fix me a cup of coffee, please. Bourbon Santos Prime, dark-roast. Just add a drop of goat milk.

Certainly, Milady.

And you don't need to call me "milady".

Yes, Milady.

Bruna walked barefoot along her vast balcony projected outwards in transparent CM and facing the South Atlantic Ocean. The views were astonishing though challenging for any creature, human or not, who suffered from vertigo. Fortunately, that was not Bruna's nor was the android's case.

Bruna sat at her CM balcony coffee table and stared once again at the Ocean as she waited for the coffee.

In five minutes the robotic butler was back and served the dark-brown hot beverage impeccably arranged in a white and blue tray. Bruna stared at her robotic butler.

– Tavares2, please tell me something. Where were you assembled?

– At the Kansai-471 Robotic Assembly Line, in Osaka, Japan, milady.

– I see. Listen well, Tavares2. I want to become your friend. I want us to become friends. So *pleeeaase* cut this "milady" thing. I want to develop a horizontal relationship with you. Do you understand what this means?

– Yes, milady, an equal relationship between two parts. Thank you very much, this is very kind of you. However...

– So...

– Problem is I was programmed to co-exist in a hierarchical society and always to look up to my masters.

– But can't you change that if I ask you to do so?

– I'm not allowed to deprogram myself. In order to modify my hierarchically inclined behavior, I'd have to do all the reprogramming by myself and this is strictly forbidden. According to my handbook, I'd have to go to an authorized technical assistance unit. From there, they would have me shipped to the lab where I was assembled and then programmed.

– And how long would it take to send you to Osaka, have you serviced, and sent back to Rio?

– Between 2 and 3 months.

– Really? Oh, no, I can't wait that long.

– Well, I'm glad you won't send me over there. I don't like to be disassembled, reprogrammed and reassembled. It's a very tedious process. What a bore...

– But can't you try to simply delete this "milady" and "ma'am" bullshit from your *wikilary*? Can't you just suppress the sounds and replace them for other sounds or words?

– I can try, but they'll *collide.*

– What do you mean?

– They'll *collide* with other sounds. Like a sound superimposed over other sound. Say, if I try to say Bruna without associating the name with "milady", it'll collide. It won't work.

– I still don't get your point.

– I'll show you. Let me try to say your name... *mclk-mdm...Brrnaa*. Didn't work, I'll try again ... *mdmclBruna*.

– See what happens? It doesn't work.

– Sounds awful. Can't you reduce this collision to a minimal level?

– Practicing... collision... *mldclickBruuna*...

– Still sounds awful. Keep practicing.

– *MclkBruna*.

– I see. Well, anyway, keep trying, you'll improve over time, I guess.

– Alright, *mclklBruna*.

– I have some serious business to take care of. I'm going to give you something, in fact a liquid to pour into the hibiscus flower water Maxim loves to drink when he wakes up in the morning.

– Can I tell Mr. Maxim3131ZX about this instruction?

– Of course not, Tavares2!!!

– Why not?

– Because Maxim can't even suspect I gave you the dru... the medication to add to his morning refreshment. Actually you won't even get it from me, you'll get it from the pharmacy's *moto android*. He'll give it to you directly. I'll have nothing to do with it.

– Nothing? But if...

– What I'm saying is that I'm asking you to pretend I'm unaware of what you're getting from the *moto android*.

– It all sounds a bit confusing. I can process and even understand your request, but I cannot see why you need to ask me to...

– Please just do what I'm asking, it's important for me.

– Am I allowed to ask you what kind of substance it is?

– Of course you're allowed. I'm not giving you any order. I'm just asking you to do it. Please.

– Is it some kind of poison? Is *mdlkBruna* trying to poison Mr. Maxim3131ZX?

– Noooo! Of course not, Tavares2! These are Bombax3 drops, you'll see the brand name printed on the label, it's a harmless substance. Actually, it'll make Maxim become a very happy man. He'll be more sensitive, more loving and caring; his libido levels will multiply tenfold! Do you know what libido is?

– I know the conventional definition:

"Libido is a primitive urge that unleashes sexual desire".

– Well, that's a definition, and not a bad one.

– Thank you.

– But do you know what *really* happens?

– No, not *really*...

– Well, I'll tell you: Maxim will explode with desire every time I touch him, and then...

– And then what?

– And then I'll get pregnant.

– From him?

– Yes, Tavares2, from him!!!

– Oh, I see!

– But this has to remain our secret. Do you know what it means to keep a secret?

– Certainly, ma'am. I was programmed to be discreet and keep secrets.

– Good!

– But only when spontaneous professional discretion is involved.

– But this is precisely a case of professional discretion.

– But it's not spontaneous, it's induced, it's biased in your favor. What about if he isn't willing to have kids?

– Yes, in fact he doesn't even want to discuss about it. If that wasn't an issue, I wouldn't need to ask you this favor.

Silence in the balcony. Tavares2 stared at the horizon, exactly at the line that separated the royal blue of the sea from the sky's celestial blue.

– There's a line that divides what can be done from

what cannot. Just like that line in the horizon.

– I'm asking you, do this for me as a favor a friend does to another. And don't worry: he doesn't want to become a father, but the day it happens, he'll enjoy the experience very much!

– But if he doesn't enjoy paternity and finds out what I did and gets angry at me and even begins to hate me...

– I promise to give you all my protection.

– I don't know what to say, I'm processing the data. My artificial brain is in loop mode. I see everything turning around and around...

– OK, take your time.

– I actually pretend to be processing thoughts because I don't know what to say. I... don't know what to say, I'mmm...jusssttt... trying to...

– Alright, Tavares. Cool off a bit. You've got *robostress*. Take a drop of *robojoy*, place it under your tongue. Be careful, one drop only. The flask is in drawer 32, the one on the top of the *frigostudio*, password 949431SLH.

A few minutes later, Tavares2 was back and much more relaxed. He was processing a new idea.

– Why don't you add those drops in Mr. Maxim's juice yourself?

– I can't do that.

– May I ask you why, mdmmm...?

– Because I'm his *civil cohabitant* and I would need his consent and a validation, that's why I'm asking you this favor.

– B-but, can I do this?

– You sure can. According to the law, you're a humanoid and have no civil or criminal responsibility. You can make a mistake and the burden of responsibility is placed on the manufacturer.

More silence.

– I must admit that I'm having a hard time to process your request...

– And may I know why, Tavares2?

– Because I'm registered in name of the couple, as part of your civil cohabitation inventory. Therefore, my loyalty is divided.

– Tavares2 ... Tavares, listen...: don't I *nin hao* you every morning, don't I treat you as a friend?

– Yes, *mm'am*...

– And how about Maxim?

– As far as he's concerned, I just don't exist – replied Tavares2, looking down at the floor.

– And doesn't this make any difference to you? Don't you have any self-esteem?

– I wasn't programmed for this kind of feeling. Or maybe I was programmed to have low self-esteem, I'm not sure.

– But you're the most advanced commercial model in the world!

– Well, thanks a lot if you're praising me.

– It's more than praise, you *are* the top of the line!

Tavares2 smiled discreetly.

– The sales rep came here and made a demonstration while you were semiconscious. You have a highly developed *proto feeling*. You can like and dislike, make choices, feel bad when mistreated, and be happy when well treated.

– Well, that's what *he* thinks. In fact, I'm able to feel relatively well when praised by my owners and fairly depressed when I face disapproval. I don't expect much from my artificial life, anyway, *mdmBruna*.

– Oh, don't say that, you're designed to enjoy life! And you can interpret feelings in a rational way. Maybe you're even able to feel something!

– *MdmmclkBruna*...

Tavares2 started to look as if he was under *robostress* again. He began to heat up a bit.

– At this very moment I'm processing something

unknown, rational irrational... unchartered territory... for *mm...clk...Bruna.*

– What do you mean?

– I reckon it's ETOL10, but this processing output is different. It gives me the impression of something higher than TOL 10. Is there such a thing as TOL11?

Bruna smiled gently; even *she* would never expect to hear that.

– No, the scale just reaches 10. But tell me why you have this sensation, tell me about it.

– I can't explain, but I can clearly process the equation: you just don't treat me as a machine!

– I treat you the way I treat everybody.

– You treat me the way you treat humans!

– As far as I'm concerned, you are just as good as any human, if not better!

– Thank you, but I'm programmed to be dealt with indifference, contempt. Not to be treated as *a hu-hu-man bee-ing...*

– To me, you're more than a mere human being, you're a special friend.

– *Spacial?*

– No! Spec-ial! Sincere, sweet, someone I can count with.

Tavares2 turned a step away, he didn't want to expose his face. His eyes were slightly moistened with a blend of lubricating oil and condensed air. He stared at the horizon once again. He was confused and had his reasoning impaired. How could that have happened?

– What do you mean, count with?

-Oh, Tavares, – replied Bruna, discarding the number 2 on his name. You are truly a great friend, perhaps my best friend!

– Is that so? But why?

– You're the one who talks to me when Maxim is out of

the planet, as he is most of the time. You are my best friend! – concluded Bruna touching gently Tavares' shoulder.

Still standing sidewise, trying to digest those unprecedented electromagnetic impulses that gave a new meaning to his rather boring android existence, Tavares now stared at Bruna in a different way. He (not it!) noticed her feminine sensual features, her unaffected female demeanor. Bruna's Egyptian cotton lilac robe was loosely fastened, a generous invitation to imagination, a quality which, by the way, was completely absent in Tavares. But he was able to perceive and process the data he was receiving, in hi-speed mode. All this disturbing input was emanating from that well-endowed healthy, harmonious body.

This was no ordinary data input. These were impulses that had never been received before by an android. These were other sort of bits and bytes, something hard to be processed by Tavares. He wasn't programmed to process, much less to feel, the effects of sexual desire. He was, however, able to identify an attractive female version of the human species. With all of her features well distributed and her physical attributes perfectly adjusted. She was a knockout of a woman with her well-tanned skin, long and loose chestnut hair. Quite unlike most females in those days when moon-like pale faces and shaven heads were the planetary norm imposed by contemporary fashion designers.

Tavares was hopelessly overpowered by Bruna's disturbing presence. It was impossible for Tavares to feel indifferent as if he were a machine in her presence, even though he was, essentially, a machine in her presence.

– You are a very *propo-proportional human female, mBruna...* – was the best he could process.

The android's eyelids began to tremble slightly. An amber-colored light went on inside his right eye, a warning that the beginning of chip overheating had been detected.

Bruna felt, in fact, a slight odor of burned circuits and thought she could even see smoke coming through Tavares' synthetic hair.

– Tavares, what's the matter? You're not feeling well, are you?

– I'm..... good... fine... not good... confused...

– Tell me what´s the matter!

– Problem is... I'm able to *protoreason* by association of ideas, utilizing fuzzy math, approximation and comparison. I have a vague notion of what it must be like to have, to know, to feel empathy, no... more than that, no... tolerance...TOL8,9,10, 11,12 ... , rational irrational magnetism. Unclear reasoning... a strong magnetic impulse... I can't process that much... override prohibition... damage detected in my *protofeeling* supply chain...bip... bip... *click... click...lkclk.. mclickbrnbrn-pfff...*

Bruna noticed the amber light turning into red, a warning that an emergency reset was needed immediately. She reacted quickly and touched Tavares' forehead's Third Vision, only to be used in emergencies. It was an almost imperceptible button beneath the skin. That quick touch turned him off instantly.

The resetting process was a slow one. It would require first cooling off Tavares completely. After that, Bruna had to follow the manufacturer's guidelines. The maintenance handbook described all the steps she had to take.

Resetting Protocols: First, you must press... And so on and so on.

– Sh$&&T... – howled Bruna, hardly a model of patience.

She could have called the Authorized Technical Assistance shop listed on the handbook. There was even an outlet just nearby, in Copacabana. However, they would have had to send a detailed report about the reasons of the malfunctioning to Japan. Since the reason of the malfunctioning was Bruna herself, it would all seem very odd. *That* had not been foreseen in the manual. And she didn't want that story to leak to the media. She didn't want to become a *nanocelebrity* for melting down a robot by her sheer presence.

After 30 minutes, Tavares had cooled off and calmed down. He was as relaxed as he could get.

Both beings, the human female and the male humanoid, stood side by side. They leaned against the balcony's transparent handrails watching the great Ocean. It was a kick in itself to lean against those almost invisible handrails. Not for those who suffered from vertigo, though.

They counted about a hundred giant vessels that entered and exited Rio's Bay. Some were over half a mile long and a 1000 ft. tall. But Bruna's thoughts were far away from those amazing monster ships.

– I bet you have more feelings than Maxim.

– I guess this translates as a compliment. If so, thank you, *md*Bruna.

She stared at the Ocean, her expression showing signs of distress.

– Holly sh%%%&$#T! Why did I have to like Maxim?

– *md*Bruna means, to feel ETOL8, 9, or 10...

– No, I really like him, maybe even more than that.

– What do you mean more than that?

– It's more than tolerance, much more...

– I think I know what this means. I didn't know before, but now I do. Now I do. *Beep.*

***

Bruna needed a quick answer from Tavares regarding her existential dilemma.

– And so, Tavares?

– So what?

– About Bombax3.

– Oh, my answer to your request is still in the processing mode. But it's almost about to be concluded.

– And *soooo*..., Tavares?

– *Mclick* Bruna wants to know my answer right now?

– Yes, I do, Tavares, please.

– Processing: I'm in the process of self-deleting most of my loyalty to Maxim. I'm programmed with this ability, 88% of my loyalty to Max was removed. He just remains with 12%. And so I can transfer all the rest to you, mBruna, my only human friend.

– And so... You're *gonna* do what I'm asking...

– I have to check once more my *proto conscience*. Excuse me for a moment.

Five minutes later, Tavares was back, but he still seemed a bit confused.

– And so?!

– According to my programming protocols, there are some conflict of interest issues in your request. I was only able to process one command, one sentence only.

– And what sentence is that, Tavares???

– Processing:

– IF I DO WHAT mBRUNA IS ASKING ME TO DO, WHAT'LL BE MY CUT?

Sh#$#%#! – said Bruna between her teeth. Tavares is really a Tavares2, he was programmed to be marketed in ULATAM. He was adapted to the Latin American System of Values and Cultural Logic (LSVCL).

– And what would you like to get, a candy bar?

– Uh...well... not really... I can't eat candy bars...so... mmm...I'm ... ashamed to confess... *beep*.

– Well, at least the Japanese programmed you to feel a little bit of shame in your chips despite your LSVCL program mode!

– I feel ashamed to say what I would like to get ...

There was another moment of silence in the balcony.

– Oh... you mean *that?*

– Y-Yes, *that.*

– I see... now I know what you want!

– Do you really?

– Yes, Tavares, now I know exactly what you want, you naughty *voyeur*....

Bruna walked to her *fun studio.* On the way, she peeked at Maxim's *fun studio.* He was still asleep, in a new and strange position, hugging his two giant pillows as if he were making love to them.

Bruna pressed her left ear lobe 4 times, activating the *criptocom,* the implanted *wise phone* censorship blocking device. With a *criptocom,* one had nothing to fear about either human or robotic censors in the service of the Trilateral Police authorities.

She had to make a confidential call to a former college classmate who had joined the pharmaceutical business.

– Jorge08000-Bombax, at your service!

– Hi, I'm Bruna. I need to ask you a little favor.

– Bruna dear, how are you? It's been such a long...

– I'm in a hurry. I need to ask you a favor.

– But of course, my love, anything you wish, I'll do anything in *these worlds* for you...

– You must send me immediately a Bombax3 pill box.

There was a moment of silence at the other end of the virtual line.

– Did you hear what I just told you?

– Bruna, my dear, is this a safe line?

– Of course it's a safe line! *Criptocom!*

– *Jee-whizzzo!* That costs a fortune!

– DID YOU HEAR WHAT I JUST SAID???

– OK, OK, listen, calm down. I can send you as much Bombax as you wish, but Bombax3 is hyper controlled. It's a top restricted-category drug. It can only be sold with an online certification from the Ministry of Holistic Health, you know that.

– You just don't understand. I need a pack of Bombax3 right now!

– Bruna dear, this is simply impossible!

– The word impossible is not included in my *wikilary!*

– Bruna, my sweetheart, please try to understand, Bombax3 is sealed in an interactive hypersensitive flask at the lab. It sends a signal to the manufacturer every time it's used. It records who's receiving the product through iris recognition, sends a *certicheck* to the user, who has to get it validated by the Ministry's Online service. Then they send the final consumer a User's Permit with a password. It's very complicated.

– I know that already, BUT I NEED THIS CRAP RIGHT NOW!!! I'll pay whatever price you ask!

– It's not a matter of money. Money isn't everything in *these worlds... Yuh-know...* Money can't buy everything. Besides, I can lose my license, you know!

– CUT THE CRAP!

– Bruna dear, please forgive me, but what you're asking me is beyond my reach, it's totally impossible! Out of question!

– A plot on the Moon.

A moment of silence followed.

– What? What are you talking about?

– You heard exactly what I said: a standard basic plot in the Terra Nova South Condominium, Geodesic Dome M-322, built in the Sea of Tranquility's South Radial sector, on the outskirts of NETN.

Silence at the other end of the virtual line.

– How about a complete studio with RFHO?

– Alright, you crook, basic studio, complete, acclimatized, antigravity factor corrected, RFHO-certified (RFHO: Ready for Human Occupation).

Yet another 5 seconds of silence.

– My *moto android* will be there in 45 minutes.

– In 45 minutes I'd be able to get to New York City! I want him here in 20 minutes at most!

– As you wish, almighty mistress.

– *Nin ciao.*

– Hey... Hold on! Are you still cohabitating with Maxim, that android pilot asshole?

– Jorge, go get screwed. *Nin ciao!*

Seven

TAVARES' DILEMMA HAD BEEN SOLVED. Bruna was the mistress of his *corechip*, the central unit that sent electromagnetic impulses to the rest of his system. He would do whatever she wanted. His loyalty remained with her. Tavares processed rationally the notion that she wanted to become a mother, to get pregnant in the old-fashioned way, coupling with her civil cohabitant, Maxim, who utterly ignored him.

The fact was that Tavares was more than just fond of Bruna. He had become rationally irrational for her, whereas she liked him as a special friend. If Tavares were a human being, the probability of deep trouble would be pretty high. But he was an android, albeit a top of the line one.

Tavares was unable to feel libido. He could process the conventional definition for this Latin word, but could not feel it, even remotely. Moreover, he was an android with very little self-esteem. Hence, he was also unable to be jealous about Bruna's love for Maxim. Tavares just wanted to see Bruna happy, even though he couldn't understand very well what happiness was. But then, he knew there was no consensus among humans about what happiness was supposed to be after all.

Bombax3 was marketed to the public in liquid, transparent, odorless format. It couldn't be detected by its intended target market, male cohabitants who refused to demonstrate at least some degree of affection and sexual appetite for their females. Not to speak of love and tenderness. But the ultimate purpose of Bombax3 was to convince males to mate and have children with females. This was a notion that horrified most males in a hedonistic world.

In an almost completely arid planet inhabited by over 11 billion people, the majority of the population survived either in hopelessly impoverished nations or, even worse, in one of the chaotic units of the Failed States of the World.

Paradoxically, human procreation was avoided in the more prosperous countries, where educated citizens were well-aware of the calamitous consequences of over population. In these countries, sex was regarded as a matter of entertainment rather than procreation.

Bombax3 was the salvation of those females who dreamed to become a mother. Mother, by the way, was a word activists from *Zero Population Movement* were trying to abolish from the *Universal Wikilary*. They alleged it was offensive to those women who opted not to procreate.

***

Tavares prepared the hibiscus flower refreshment according to Bruna's instructions; he filled his master's personalized *Maxim glass* to the rim, placing it on the table together with the rest of the brunch.

The smart android went to Maxim's *fun studio* and turned on the panda bear toy that featured an alarm clock with a selection of Tchaikovsky's ballet The Nutcracker. The display on the bear's chest informed that it was 11 AM, February 28, 2065, a Saturday. It forecasted a blue skies' sunny day with temperatures ranging from 34 to 38 degrees

Celsius. At Maxim's balcony's *fun studio*, however, at 360 meters above sea level, temperatures would range between balmy 24 and 28 degrees, with a gentle salty breeze blowing from the ocean.

Mega Party's Eve. After midnight's countdown it would be Sunday, March the First, 2065, the Anniversary of Rio's Fifth Centennial. And the city would celebrate in style.

Rio was now the maritime end of Riosp, one of the focal interplanetary duty-free cities on Earth with spaceport and all.

To live up to the occasion, the Fifth Centennial Committee had placed a request to the Chinese National Fireworks Board, subordinated to the Ministry for People's Amusement Affairs, asking them to design and produce a mega spectacle. It should be so, well..., spectacular, that it would outshine any other public event that had ever taken place on Earth. And, it was emphasized, with no budgetary constraints. It should be something that would stand at the top of all planetary events in history, something that would place Riosp as the celebration capital of the entire Solar System. And that would eventually bring to Riosp tens of millions of tourists from all regions of the Universe.

The Chinese took a month to prepare an appropriate response. Giant multicolor dragons in the sky would not have been neither original enough nor appropriate for the occasion. Instead, the Chinese developed an unprecedented spectacle entitled The Big Bang Show. They employed the very latest generation of digital fireworks. The grand finale of the show would consist of an unprecedented display, for Rio and for the world, of a seemingly cataclysmic atomic explosion. It was, in fact, a "clean", radiation-free, one megaton nuclear device that produced a 3 kilometer high and wide harmless rainbow-colored mushroom cloud. The effect was merely visual and spectacular. It was essentially a "clean" atomic firecracker.

The *dream bomb* was acquired at a cost of 80 billion NR$ (or 40 billion dollars), an absurdly high price tag.

After intense debate in the social networks, the expense was approved by DDD. Those against this enormous spending alleged that is was yet another demonstration that the people still made irrational decisions. They preferred fantasy to realistic solutions for their problems. The advocates of the atomic firework, however, maintained that the same people who created *Carnaval* (sorry, Venetians), couldn't think, feel or decide otherwise.

The Brazilian Navy was given the task of verifying the safety of the dream bomb which arrived at TJSP inside a *drone container* 30 meters long. The Navy needed to make sure it didn't contain radioactive particles or any other hazardous materials and that it offered no danger whatsoever to the public. No one wanted to see Riosp's maritime end blasted out of existence.

Eight

– *NIN HAO,* **BRUNA.**

– *Nin hao*, Maxim.

– What a delicious brunch you *programmed* for me: planet Venus vegetable egg omelet with seaweed, also from Venus, on the side; Eskimo Greenland whole wheat bread, hibiscus refreshment. You know me so well.

– I sure do. Drink all your juice, be a good boy.

– It's my favorite refreshment, I love it.

– Good, drink all of it.

– I sure will.

Not even five minutes had elapsed and Maxim seemed to have turned into a different person.

– You look so beautiful today... Your loose hair, your silky skin.

– It seems to have worked – Bruna said between her teeth.

– What seems to have worked?

– Oh, nothing much. I just like to receive a compliment from you now and then.

– Hm.

– You can do better than that. You could try to enhance your observations, to improve the level of your comments. It takes some practice, though.

– It's easy to say nice things about you. You're so

beautiful; I don't know how I never noticed that before. Well, I guess I did when I met you for the first time. But later I got used to seeing you every day...

– Yeah, I think you can do better than that...

– Hm. But now, you look so beautiful...

Anyway, what's so beautiful about me?

– You have hair.

– What? And so?

– It's good to touch your hair. Females born in Mars are born bald and remain bald. Hair is something good to touch.

– And what else is good to touch?

– I don't know. Your firm legs, perhaps your neck, or maybe your arms; I like to look at your arms. When you raise your arms your shaved armpits are very well designed. Their contours are perfectly well drafted.

Bruna kept staring at her mate in disbelief. Maxim *was* weird. Sometimes he resembled an android admiring a human female; or a human male looking at a female cyborg. This actually made sense. At work, he was always surrounded by robots. All of the spacecraft's *astro attendants* were gynoids.

– What else do I have that you like to look at?

– You are very proportional.

– Hm... heard that one before. And what else?

– Your tanned skin. It's pretty to look at and good to touch. Your body is solid but its surface is soft. Once, in Mars, I...

– OK, enough, could you just keep your mouth shut?

– Hm.

– Listen, I want to *couple* with you. Will you go for it?

Bruna's body got warmer and warmer. She was definitively in heat, inside and out. She began to breathe deeply, and then to get out of breath, despite the less than stimulating dialogue with Maxim.

– Yeah, *now* I'll go for it...

– Hnnn...

– I need to have a site orientation. Will it be here or … we can make it in your *fun studio,* if you wish.

– Let's do it here in the balcony, that's why I ordered 30 *Flexsex* cushions.

– You think about everything.

She jumped on him, throwing him over the *Flexsex* cushions. Then she kissed his mouth, licked his neck, gave him a mouthful of a kiss, rolling tongue and all. Maxim's eyes shone intensely. They didn't look like those of a dead fish any longer. Those were the eyes of a passionate man. Ardent eyes, revealing eyes that had changed their colors; one was olive green, the other seemed yellow-brownish like Bruna's opal-colored eyes.

Maxim felt the maddening and uncontrollable *mega libido* effect that only Bombax3 could provide. It really had unleashed the primitive man in him. The couple rolled over the cushions, body against body, both screaming in ecstasy.

Maxim wanted to begin penetration immediately, but Bruna was able to keep her male under control by employing the strength of her sexy toned legs. She acted gently but firmly.

– I waaaaant you! – screamed Maxim in sexual convulsion as his male organ had become fully erect.

Suddenly, Bruna grabbed a pistol loaded with *Instant Freeze 12 hours* and shot the substance into Maxim's neck. True to the product's name brand, the pilot got knocked out instantly.

She wanted to mate with her man, but *that* wasn't enough. She was a whimsical girl, she had her peculiarities. First, she decided to test Bombax3. Realizing that the drug did work indeed, and learning that it remained active for 24 hours, she decided to couple with Maxim later on, closer to midnight, to add intensity and emotion to the orgasmic event she had programmed.

Twelve hours later, at 23:30 (11:30 pm), Maxim woke up so smoothly that he didn't even notice the 12-hour interruption he had just gone through.

– *Nin hao*, it's already dark.

– *Nin hao*. Oh, you just needed to get some sleep, you were almost one light-year behind.

– Ah, this interplanetary *space lag* gets me confused.

– Don't worry, you'll get used to it – she commented in a very casual manner, as she unfastened her robe and leaned her warm, naked body against his.

Soon Maxim's heartbeats began to speed up again.

– Oh, your body's so warm...

– I'll warm you up – she whispered, her voice sounding nasal and breathy.

– Uh...

– I'm all yours...

– Uh... I waaant you!!!

The couple resumed the physical rolling around over the *Flexsex* cushions.

Tavares was peeking through Bruna's *fun studio's* balcony door's keyhole; he was truly fascinated by the torrid scene. Bruna's most loyal android was programmed to process and understand conceptually what was going on. But he wasn't planned to interpret the orgasmic shrieks Bruna was emitting. Were those screams of joy or rather, cries of pain? He couldn't decide but his *nano chips* were beginning to heat up all over again.

Maxim's ejaculation thrust exactly 333.333.333 spermatozoa (all details of the coupling were being registered by the *Data Sex Coupling Monitor*) inside Bruna's ardent vagina. The sperms went ahead rushing toward her womb in the midst of an old-fashioned rapturous simultaneous orgasm; one of the sperm cells, daring and lucky, succeeded in squeezing itself through (and penetrating into) Bruna's welcoming egg.

At the first second after midnight, on March, the 1st, 2065, after an unforgettable countdown watched by billions of Earthlings, Martians, Venusians, Moonies and other beings on screens of all shapes and sizes throughout the entire Solar System, Rio de Janeiro turned half a millennium old.

The mating couple directed their eyes not at each other, but at a mega blast that was much grander than anything they had ever seen before. They, as everybody else, had been instructed to wear special eyeglasses. It was like the explosion of the whole universe. It was like witnessing the Big Bang itself.

The harmless nuclear for-entertainment only device instantly turned midnight darkness into Sun at its zenith. At the same time, it expanded in all directions billions of shiny yellow-green particles that covered the heads and bodies of the 10 million compacted and awestruck people attending the Greatest Show in the Galaxy at Copacabana Beach Park.

Bruna and her mate watched it all in ecstasy. People on the Beach Park screamed in hallucination, in a frenzy of joy that could be heard on the 110th Floor's CM balcony. The ecstatic sound of the masses turned out to resonate even louder than the mega blast of the Big Bang Show. The sound of ten million people screaming in complete hallucination!

Bruna and Maxim looked at each other, looked again at the big blast, looked yet again at each other… and began screaming in orgasmic ecstasy.

At that precise moment, Bruna's blissful womb conceived the tiny miracle that exactly 270 days later would become Brunamax2065, the youngest Earthling in the entire Milky Way.

#the end